Making Music

Written by Dana Meachen Rau
Illustrated by Maureen Ivy Fisher

Reading Advisers:

Gail Saunders-Smith, Ph.D., Reading Specialist

*Dr. Linda D. Labbo, Department of Reading Education,
College of Education, The University of Georgia*

LEVEL B

A COMPASS POINT
EARLY READER

For Derek

A Note to Parents

As you share this book with your child, you are showing your new reader what reading looks like and sounds like. You can read to your child anywhere—in a special area in your home, at the library, on the bus, or in the car. Your child will associate reading with the pleasure of being with you.

This book will introduce your young reader to many of the basic concepts, skills, and vocabulary necessary for successful reading. Talk through the details in each picture before you read. Then read the book to your child. As you read, point to each word, stopping to talk about what the words mean and the pictures show. Your child will begin to link the sounds of the letters with the look of the words that you and he or she read.

After your child is familiar with the story, let him or her read the story alone. Be careful to let the young reader make mistakes and correct them on his or her own. Be sure to praise the young reader's abilities. And, above all, have fun.

Gail Saunders-Smith, Ph.D.
Reading Specialist

Compass Point Books
3722 West 50th Street, #115
Minneapolis, MN 55410

Visit Compass Point Books on the Internet at *www.compasspointbooks.com* or e-mail your request to *custserv@compasspointbooks.com*

Library of Congress Cataloging-in-Publication Data
Rau, Dana Meachen, 1971–
    Making music / written by Dana Meachen Rau ; illustrated by Maureen Ivy Fisher.
    p. cm. — (Compass Point early reader)
    "Level B."
    Summary: Uses sound words to introduce music and types of musical instruments, continuing to add more and more instruments until a band is formed.
    ISBN 0-7565-0118-0
    1. Musical instruments—Juvenile literature. [1. Musical instruments.] I. Fisher, Maureen Ivy, ill. II. Title. III. Series.
ML460 .R32 2002
784—dc21   2001002676

Bang! Rumble!

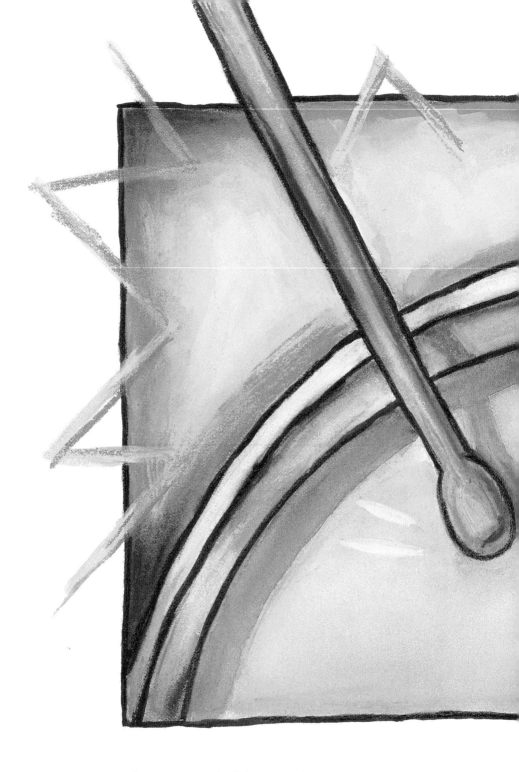

Tum! Tum! Tum!

4

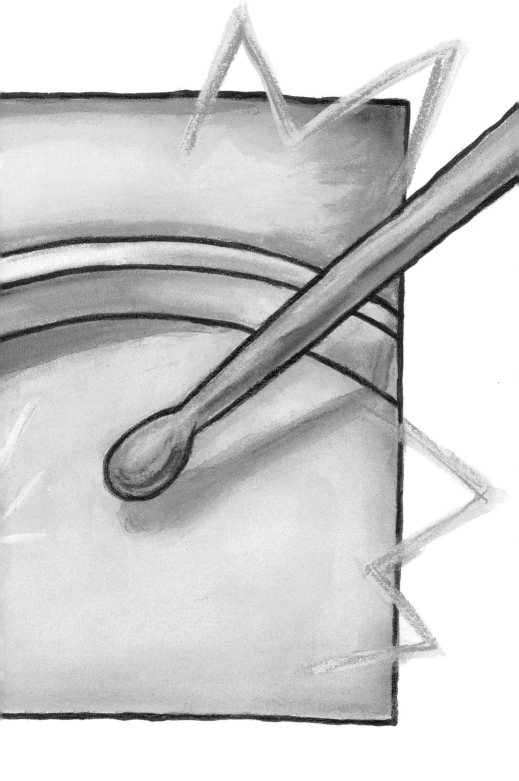

That's what I hear when
Tom beats the drum.

Blurt! Bellow!

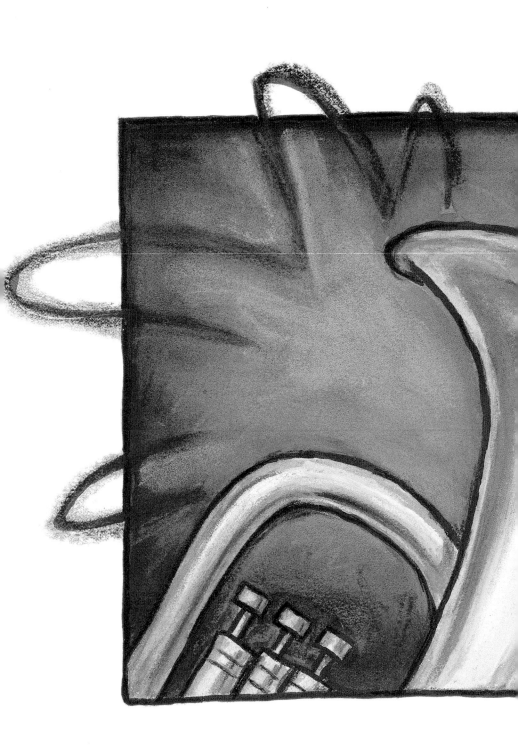

Boom! Boo! Ba!

11

That's what I hear when

Sue blows the tuba.

Doo. Doo. Dee. Dee.

15

Toot! Toot! Toot!

That's what I hear when

Pete plays the flute.

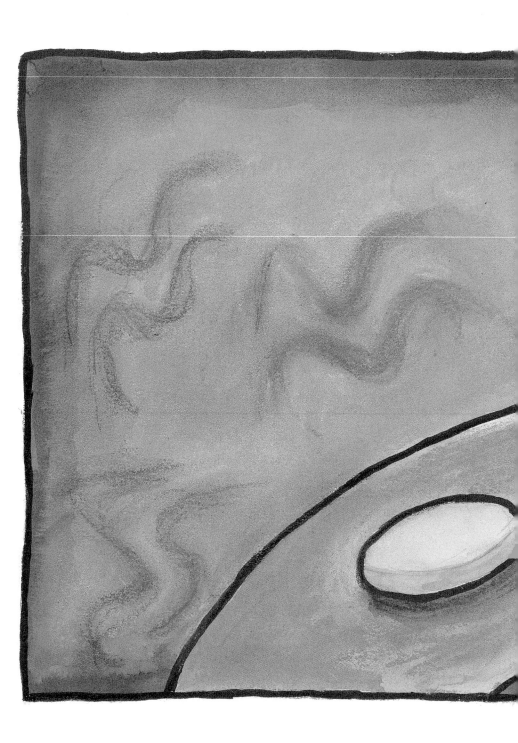

Zing. Twang.

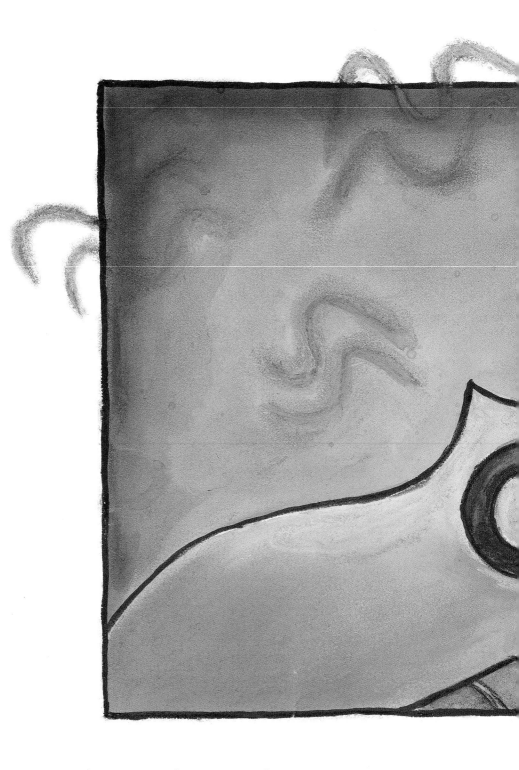

Ping! Ping! Ping!

That's what I hear when

Lynn strums a string.

Bravo! Good job!

Yay! Hooray!

That's what the orchestra

hears after they play.

More Fun with Music!

Ask your child if he or she has ever heard a band play. Perhaps he or she has been to a concert or a parade. Tell your child that there are many different kinds of instruments, and they all make different sounds.

Try asking your child the following questions:

• You hit a drum to make a noise. What other instruments must be hit?

• You blow into a tuba or a flute to make sound. What other instruments do people blow?

• You strum or use a bow on the strings of a violin to play a tune. What other instruments have strings?

Ask your child to think of other objects that can be instruments too. A rubber band around a box makes a funny noise. An empty jar filled with beans sounds like a rattle. Remind your child that bodies are also instruments. When you clap your hands or whistle, you are making music!

Word List

(In this book: 43 words)

a	good	Sue
after	hear	that's
ba	hears	the
bang	hooray	they
beats	I	Tom
bellow	job	toot
blows	Lynn	tuba
blurt	orchestra	tum
boo	Pete	twang
boom	ping	what
bravo	play	when
dee	plays	yay
doo	rumble	zing
drum	string	
flute	strums	

About the Author

When Dana Meachen Rau was little, she would scare easily. Every time she went to a parade, she covered her ears because she thought the marching band was too loud. Then one day she forgot to cover them and realized that the music was actually fun to listen to, especially the drums. Dana isn't very good at playing instruments and has a terrible singing voice, so that is why she sticks to writing. But she loves to listen to music with her husband Chris and son Charlie in Farmington, Connecticut.

About the Illustrator

Maureen Ivy Fisher was a little girl when she started to draw. Her dad is an artist and she wanted to grow up to be just like him. So she drew and painted all the time. Now she makes pictures for children's books. Making art makes Ms. Fisher look closely at things and see how they're put together. She lives and paints happily in Wheeling, Illinois, with her husband Ernie, her son Mackie, stepchildren Jake and Sarah, and dog Callie.